The
Truth
Is a Cave
in the Black
Mountains

ALSO BY NEIL GAIMAN

FOR ADULTS

The Ocean at the End of the Lane

Stories (edited with Al Sarrantonio)

Fragile Things

Anansi Boys

American Gods

Stardust

Smoke and Mirrors

Neverwhere

Good Omens (with Terry Pratchett)

FOR ALL AGES

The Graveyard Book (illustrated by Dave McKean)

M Is for Magic

Coraline (illustrated by Dave McKean)

Odd and the Frost Giants (illustrated by Brett Helquist)

Crazy Hair (illustrated by Dave McKean)

Blueberry Girl (illustrated by Charles Vess)

The Dangerous Alphabet (illustrated by Chris Grimly)

The Day I Swapped My Dad for Two Goldfish (illustrated by Dave McKean)

The Wolves in the Walls (illustrated by Dave McKean)

The Truth
Is a Cave
in the Black
Mountains

A Tale of Travel and Darkness
with Pictures of All Kinds

WRITTEN BY NEIL GAIMAN
WITH ILLUSTRATIONS BY EDDIE CAMPBELL

headline

First published in Great Britain in 2014
by HEADLINE PUBLISHING GROUP

Cataloguing in Publication Data is available from the British Library

ISBN 978 1 4722 2107 0 (Hardback)

Printed in Italy

Headline's policy is to use papers that are natural, renewable and recyclable products and
made from wood grown in sustainable forests. The logging and manufacturing processes are
expected to conform to the environmental regulations of the country of origin.

HEADLINE PUBLISHING GROUP
An Hachette UK Company
338 Euston Road
London NW1 3BH

www.headline.co.uk
www.hachette.co.uk

Shortly after I fell in love with the Isle of Skye, I discovered the books of the late Otta F. Swire, books on the legends and history of the Inner and Outer Hebrides. This book started with a sentence in one of her books, and grew around it. This book is for her, and all my living friends on the Island, particularly for George McKain, and for Willie, Johnnie, and the entire Nicolson family, a small exchange for many tumblers of whisky, cups of tea, and boat journeys.

You ask me if I can forgive myself?

I can forgive myself for many things. For where I left him. For what I did. But I will not forgive myself for the year that I hated my daughter, when I believed her to have run away, perhaps to the city. During that year I forbade her name to be mentioned, and if her name entered my prayers when I prayed, it was to ask that she would one day learn the meaning of what she had done, of the dishonour that she had brought to my family, of the red that ringed her mother's eyes.

I hate myself for that, and nothing will ease that, not even what happened that night, on the side of the mountain.

I had searched for nearly ten years, although the trail was cold. I would say that I found him by accident, but I do not believe in accidents. If you walk the path, eventually you must arrive at the cave.

But that was later. First, there was the valley on the mainland, the whitewashed house in the gentle meadow with the burn splashing through it, a house that sat like a square of white sky against the green of the grass and the heather just beginning to purple.

And there was a boy outside the house, picking wool from off a thorn-bush. He did not see me approaching, and he did not look up until I said, "I used to do that. Gather the wool from the thorn-bushes and twigs. My mother would wash it, then she would make me things with it. A ball, and a doll."

He turned. He looked
shocked, as if I had appeared out
of nowhere. And I had not. I had
walked many a mile, and had many
more miles to go. I said, "I walk
quietly. Is this the house of Calum
MacInnes?"

The boy nodded, drew himself
up to his full height, which was
perhaps two fingers bigger than
mine, and he said, "I am Calum
MacInnes."

"Is there another of that name?
For the Calum MacInnes that I seek
is a grown man."

The boy said nothing, just
unknotted a thick clump of sheep's
wool from the clutching fingers
of the thorn-bush. I said, "Your
father, perhaps? Would he be Calum
MacInnes as well?"

The boy was peering at me.
"What are you?" he asked.

And I saw a smile start at the tips of his lips. "It's not a bad thing to be small, young Calum. There was a night when the Campbells came knocking on my door, a whole troop of them, twelve men with knives and sticks, and they demanded of my wife, Morag, that she produce me, as they were there to kill me, in revenge for some imagined slight. And she said, 'Young Johnnie, run down to the far meadow, and tell your father to come back to the house, that I sent for him.' And the Campbells watched as the boy ran out the door. They knew that I was a most dangerous person. But nobody had told them that I was a wee man, or if that had been told them, it had not been believed."

"Did the boy call you?" said the lad.

"It was no boy," I told him, "but me myself, it was. And they'd had me, and still I walked out the door and through their fingers."

The boy laughed. Then he said, "Why were the Campbells after you?"

"It was a disagreement about the ownership of cattle. They thought the cows were theirs. I maintained the Campbells' ownership of them had ended the first night the cows had come with me over the hills."

"Wait here," said young Calum MacInnes.

I sat by the burn and looked up at the house. It was a good-sized house: I would have taken it for the house of a doctor or a man of law, not of a border reaver. There were pebbles on the ground and I made a pile of them, and I tossed the pebbles, one by one, into the burn. I have a good eye, and I enjoyed rattling the pebbles over the meadow and into the water.

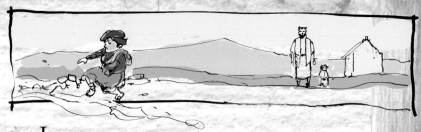

I had thrown a hundred stones when the boy returned, accompanied by a tall, loping man. His hair was streaked with grey, his face was long and wolfish. There are no wolves in those hills, not any longer, and the bears have gone too.

"Good day to you," I said.

He said nothing in return, only stared; I am used to stares. I said, "I am seeking Calum MacInnes. If you are he, say so, I will greet you. If you are not he, tell me now, and I will be on my way."

"What business would you have with Calum MacInnes?"

"I wish to hire him, as a guide."

"And where is it you would wish to be taken?"

I stared at him. "That is hard to say," I told him. "For there are some who say it does not exist. There is a certain cave on the Misty Isle."

He said nothing. Then he said, "Calum, go back to the house."

"But da—"

"Tell your mother I said she was to give you some tablet. You like that. Go on."

Expressions crossed the boy's face—puzzlement, hunger, happiness—and then he turned and ran back to the white house.

Calum MacInnes said, "Who sent you here?"

I pointed to the burn as it splashed its way between us on its journey down the hill.

I did not know him then at all, and never knew him well, but his eyes became guarded, and his head cocked to one side.

He looked me up and down, and I waited for the joke about my size, but he did not make it, and for that I was grateful.

He just said, "When we reach the cave, I will not go inside. You must bring out the gold yourself."

I said, "It is all one to me."

He said, "You can only take what you carry. I will not touch it. But yes, I will take you."

I said, "You will be paid well for your trouble." I reached into my jerkin, handed him the pouch I had in there. "This for taking me. Another, twice the size, when we return."

He poured the coins from the pouch into his huge hand, and he nodded. "Silver," he said. "Good." Then, "I will say good-bye to my wife and son."

"Is there nothing you need to bring?"

He said, "I was a reaver in my youth, and reavers travel light. I'll bring a rope, for the mountains." He patted his dirk, which hung from his belt, and went back into the whitewashed house. I never saw his wife, not then, nor at any other time. I do not know what colour her hair was.

I threw another fifty stones into the burn as I waited, until he returned, with a coil of rope thrown over one shoulder, and then we walked together away from a house too grand for any reaver, and we headed west.

The mountains between the rest of the world and the coast are gradual hills, visible from a distance as gentle, purple, hazy things, like clouds. They seem inviting. They are slow mountains, the kind you can walk up easily, like walking up a hill, but they are hills that take a full day and more to climb. We walked up the hill, and by the end of the first day we were cold.

I saw snow on the peaks above us, although it was high summer.

We said nothing to each other that first day. There was nothing to be said. We knew where we were going.

We made a fire, from dried sheep dung and a dead thorn-bush: we boiled water and made our porridge, each of us throwing a handful of oats and a fingerpinch of salt into the little pan I carried. His handful was huge, and my handful was small, like my hands, which made him smile and say, "I hope you will not be eating half of the porridge."

I said I would not and indeed, I did not, for my appetite is smaller than that of a full-grown man. But this is a good thing, I believe, for I can keep going in the wild on nuts and berries that would not keep a bigger person from starving.

A path of sorts ran across the high hills, and we followed it and encountered almost nobody: a tinker and his donkey, piled high with old pots, and a girl leading the donke who smiled at me when she thought me to be a child, and the scowled when she perceived me to be what I am, and would have thrown a stone at me had the tinker not slapped her han with the switch he had been using to encourage the donkey; and, later, we overtook an old woman and a man she said was her grandson, on their way back across the hills. We ate with her, and she told us that she had attended the birth of her first great-grandchild, that it was a good birth. She said she would tell our fortunes from the lines in our palms, if we had coins t cross her palm. I gave the old biddy a clipped lowland groat, and she looked at my palm.

She said, "I see death in your past and death in your future."

"Death waits in all our futures," I said.

She paused, there in the highest of the high lands, where the summer winds have winter on their breath, where they howl and whip and slash the air like knives. She said, "There was a woman in a tree. There will be a man in a tree."

I said, "Will this mean anything to me?"

"One day, perhaps." She said, "Beware of gold. Silver is your friend." And then she was done with me.

To Calum MacInnes she said, "Your palm has been burned." He said that was true. She said, "Give me your other hand, your left hand." He did so. She gazed at it, intently. Then, "You return to where you began. You will be higher than most other men. And there is no grave waiting for you, where you are going."

He said, "You tell me that I will not die?"

"It is a left-handed fortune. I know what I have told you, and no more."

She knew more. I saw it in her face.

That was the only thing of any importance that occurred to us on the second day.

We slept in the open that night. The night was clear and cold, and the sky was hung with stars that seemed so bright and close I felt as if I could have reached out my arm and gathered them, like berries.

We lay side by side beneath the stars, and Calum MacInnes said, "Death awaits you, she said. But death does not wait for me. I think mine was the better fortune."

"Perhaps."

"Ah," he said. "It is all a nonsense. Old-woman talk. It is not the truth."

I woke in the dawn mist to see a stag, watching us, curiously.

The third day we crested those mountains, and we began to walk downhill.

My companion said, "When I was a boy, my father's dirk fell into the cooking fire. I pulled it out, but the metal hilt was as hot as the flames. I did not expect this, but I would not let the dirk go. I carried it away from the fire, and plunged the sword into the water. It made steam. I remember that. My palm was burned, and my hand curled, as if it was meant to carry a sword until the end of time."

I said, "You, with your hand. Me, only a little man. It's fine heroes we are, who seek our fortunes on the Misty Isle."

He barked a laugh, short and without humour. "Fine heroes," was all he said.

The rain began to fall then, and did not stop falling. That night we passed a small croft-house. There was a trickle of smoke from its chimney, and we called out for the owner, but there was no response.

I pushed open the door and called again. The place was dark, but I could smell tallow, as if a candle had been burning and had recently been snuffed.

"No one at home," said Calum, but I shook my head and walked forward, then leaned my head down into the darkness beneath the bed.

"Would you care to come out?" I asked. "For we are travellers, seeking warmth and shelter and hospitality. We would share with you our oats and our salt and our whisky. And we will not harm you."

At first the woman, hidden beneath the bed, said nothing, and then she said, "My husband is away in the hills. He told me to hide myself away if the strangers come, for fear of what they might do to me."

I said, "I am but a little man, good lady, no bigger than a child, you could send me flying with a blow. My companion is a full-sized man, but I do swear that he shall do nothing to you, save partake of your hospitality, and dry ourselves. Please do come out."

All covered with dust and spiderwebs she was when she emerged, but even with her face all begrimed, she was beautiful, and even with her hair all webbed and greyed with dust it was still long and thick, and golden red. For a heartbeat she put me in the mind of my daughter, but that my daughter would look a man in the eye, while this one glanced only at the ground fearfully, like something expecting to be beaten.

I gave her some of our oats, and Calum produced strips of dried meat from his pocket, and she went out to the field and returned with a pair of scrawny turnips, and she prepared food for the three of us.

I ate my fill. She had no appetite. I believe that Calum was still hungry when his meal was done. He poured whisky for the three of us: she took but a little, and that with water. The rain rattled on the roof of the house, and dripped in the corner, and, unwelcoming though it was, I was glad that I was inside.

It was then that a man came through the door. He said nothing, only stared at us, untrusting, angry. He pulled off his cape of oiled sacking, and his hat, and he dropped them on the earth floor. They dripped and puddled. The silence was oppressive.

Calum MacInnes said, "Your wife gave us hospitality, when we found her. Hard enough she was in the finding."

"We asked for hospitality," I said. "As we ask it of you."

The man said nothing, only grunted.

In the high lands, people spend words as if they were golden coins. But the custom is strong there: strangers who ask for hospitality must be granted it, though you have blood feud against them and their clan or kind.

The woman—little more than a girl she was, while her husband's beard was grey and white, so I wondered if she was his daughter for a moment, but no: there was but one bed, scarcely big enough for two—the woman went outside, into the sheep pen that adjoined the house, and returned with oatcakes and a dried ham she must have hidden there, which she sliced thin, and placed on a wooden trencher before the man.

Calum poured the man whisky, and said,

We seek the Misty Isle. Do you know if it is there?

The man looked at us. The winds are bitter in the high lands, and they would whip the words from a man's lips. He pursed his mouth, then he said,

Aye, I saw it from the peak this morning. It's there. I cannot say if it will be there tomorrow.

We slept on the hard-earth floor of that cottage. The fire went out, and there was no warmth from the hearth. The man and his woman slept in their bed, behind the curtain. He had his way with her, beneath the sheepskin that covered that bed, and before he did that, he beat her for feeding us and for letting us in. I heard them, and could not stop hearing them, and sleep was hard in the finding that night.

I have slept in the homes of the poor, and I have slept in palaces, and I have slept beneath the stars, and would have told you before that night that all places were one to me. But I woke before first light, convinced we had to be gone from that place, but not knowing why, and I woke Calum by putting a finger to his lips, and silently we left that croft on the mountainside without saying our farewells, and I have never been more pleased to be gone from anywhere.

We were a mile from the place when I said,

We walked down a path worn by hundreds of years of sheep and deer and few enough men.

He said, "They also call it the Winged Isle. Some say it is because the island, if seen from above, would look like butterfly wings. And I do not know the truth of it." Then, "'And what is truth?' said jesting Pilate."

It is harder coming down than it is going up.

I thought about it. "Sometimes I think that truth is a place. In my mind, it is like a city: there can be a hundred roads, a thousand paths, that will all take you, eventually, to the same place. It does not matter where you come from. If you walk toward the truth, you will reach it, whatever path you take."

Calum MacInnes looked down at me and said nothing. Then,

You are wrong. The truth is a cave in the black mountains.

There is one way there, and one way only, and that way is treacherous and hard.

And if you choose the wrong path you will die alone, on the mountainside.

We crested the ridge, and we looked down to the coast. I could see villages below, beside the water. And I could see high black mountains before me, on the other side of the sea, coming out of the mist.

Calum said, "There's your cave, in those mountains."

The bones of the earth, I thought, seeing them. And then I became uncomfortable, thinking of bones, and to distract myself, I said,

And how many times is it you have been there?

Only once. I searched for it all my sixteenth year, for I had heard the legends and believed if I sought I should find.

I was seventeen when I reached it, and brought back all the gold coins I could carry.

And were you not frightened of the curse? When I was young, I was afraid of nothing

What did you do with your gold? A portion I buried and I alone know where.

The rest I used as bride-price for the woman I loved.

He stopped as if he had already said too much.

There was no ferryman at the jetty. Only a small boat, hardly big enough for three full-sized men, tied to a tree trunk on the shore, twisted and half dead, and a bell beside it.

I sounded the bell, and soon enough a fat man came down the shore.

He said to Calum, "It will cost you a shilling for the ferry, and your boy, three pennies."

I stood tall. I am not as big as other men are, but I have as much pride as any of them. "I am also a man," I said. "I'll pay your shilling."

The ferryman looked me up and down, then he scratched his beard. "I beg your pardon. My eyes are not what they once were. I shall take you to the island."

I handed him a shilling. He weighed it in his hand, "That's ninepence you did not cheat me out of. Nine pennies are a lot of money in this dark age."

The water was the colour of slate, although the sky was blue, and whitecaps chased one another across the water's surface. He untied the boat and hauled it, rattling, down the shingle to the water. We waded out into the cold water, and clambered inside.

The splash of oars on seawater, and the boat propelled forward in easy movements. I sat closest to the ferryman. I said, "Ninepence. It is good wages. But I have heard of a cave in the mountains on the Misty Isle, filled with gold coins, the treasure of the ancients."

He shook his head dismissively.

Calum was staring at me, lips pressed together so hard they were white. I ignored him and asked the man again, "A cave filled with golden coins, a gift from the Norsemen or the Southerners or from those who they say were here long before any of us: those who fled into the West as the people came."

"Heard of it," said the ferryman. "Heard also of the curse of it. I reckon that the one can take care of the other." He spat into the sea. Then he said, "You're an honest man, dwarf. I see it in your face. Do not seek this cave. No good can come of it."

"I am sure you are right," I told him, without guile.

"I am certain I am," he said. "For not every day is it that I take a reaver and a little dwarfy man to the Misty Isle." Then he said, "In this part of the world, it is not considered lucky to talk about those who went to the West." We rode the rest of the boat journey in silence, though the sea became choppier, and the waves splashed into the side of the boat, such that I held on with both hands for fear of being swept away.

29

And after what seemed like half a lifetime the boat was tied to a long jetty of black stones. We walked the jetty as the waves crashed around us, the salt spray kissing our faces. There was a humpbacked man at the landing selling oatcakes and plums dried until they were almost stones. I gave him a penny and filled my jerkin pockets with them.

We walked on into the Misty Isle.

I am old now, or at least, I am no longer young, and everything I see reminds me of something else I've seen, such that I see nothing for the first time. A bonny girl, her hair fiery-red, reminds me only of another hundred such lasses, and their mothers, and what they were as they grew, and what they looked like when they died. It is the curse of age, that all things are reflections of other things.

I say that, but my time on the Misty Isle, that is also called, by the wise, the Winged Isle, reminds me of nothing but itself.

It is a day from that jetty until you reach the black mountains.

Calum MacInnes looked at me, half his size or less, and he set off at a loping stride, as if challenging me to keep up. His legs propelled him across the ground, which was wet, and all ferns and heather.

Above us, low clouds were scudding, grey and white and black, hiding each other and revealing and hiding again.

I let him get ahead of me, let him press on into the rain, until he was swallowed by the wet, grey haze. Then, and only then, I ran.

This is one of the secret things of me, the things I have not revealed to any person, save to Morag, my wife, and Johnnie and James, my sons, and Flora, my daughter (may the Shadows rest her poor soul): I can run, and I can run well, and, if I need to, I can run faster and longer and more sure-footedly than any full-sized man; and it was like this that I ran then, through the mist and the rain, taking to the high ground and the black-rock ridges, yet keeping below the skyline.

He was ahead of me, but I spied him soon, and I ran on and I ran past him, on the high ground, with the brow of the hill between us. Below us was a stream. I can run for days without stopping. That is the first of my secrets, but there is one secret I have revealed to no man.

We had discussed already where we would camp that first night on the Misty Isle, and Calum had told me that we would spend the night beneath the rock that is called Man and Dog, for it is said that it looks like an old man with his dog by his side, and I reached it late in the afternoon. There was a shelter beneath the rock, which was protected and dry, and some of those who had been before us had left firewood behind, sticks and twigs and branches. I made a fire and dried myself in front of it and took the chill from my bones. The woodsmoke blew out across the heather.

It was dark when Calum loped into the shelter and looked at me as if he had not expected to see me that side of midnight. I said, "What took you so long, Calum MacInnes?"

He said nothing, only stared at me. I said, "There is trout, boiled in mountain water, and a fire to warm your bones."

He nodded. We ate the trout, drank whisky to warm ourselves. There was a mound of heather and of ferns, dried and brown, piled high in the rear of the shelter, and we slept upon that, wrapped tight in our damp cloaks.

I woke in the night.

There was cold steel against my throat—the flat of the blade, not the edge. I said, "And why would you ever kill me in the night, Calum MacInnes? For our way is long, and our journey is not yet over."

He said, "I do not trust you, dwarf."

"It is not me you must trust," I told him, "but those that I serve. And if you left with me but return without me, there are those who will know the name of Calum MacInnes, and cause it to be spoken in the shadows."

The cold blade remained at my throat. He said, "How did you get ahead of me?"

"And here was I, repaying ill with good, for I made you food and a fire. I am a hard man to lose, Calum MacInnes, and it ill becomes a guide to do as you did today. Now, take your dirk from my throat and let me sleep."

He said nothing, but after a few moments, the blade was removed. I forced myself neither to sigh nor to breathe, hoping he could not hear my heart pounding in my chest; and I slept no more that night.

For breakfast, I made porridge, and threw in some dried plums to soften them.

The mountains were black and grey against the white of the sky. We saw eagles, huge and ragged of wing, circling above us. Calum set a sober pace and I walked beside him, taking two steps for every one of his.

"How long?" I asked him.

"A day. Perhaps two. It depends upon the weather. If the clouds come down then two days, or even three . . ."

The clouds came down at noon and the world was blanketed by a mist that was worse than rain: droplets of water hung in the air, soaked our clothes and our skin; the rocks we walked upon became treacherous and Calum and I slowed in our ascent, stepped carefully. We were walking up the mountain, not climbing, up goat paths and craggy sharp ways. The rocks were black and slippery: we walked, and climbed and clambered and clung, we slipped and slid and stumbled and staggered, and even in the mist, Calum knew where he was going, and I followed him.

He paused at a waterfall that splashed across our path, thick as the trunk of an oak. He took the thin rope from his shoulders, wrapped it about a rock.

"This was not here before," he told me. "I'll go first." He tied one end of the rope about his waist and edged out along the path, into the falling water, pressing his body against the wet rock-face, edging slowly, intently through the sheet of water.

I was scared for him, scared for both of us: holding my breath as he passed, only breathing when he was on the other side of the waterfall. He tested the rope, pulled on it, motioned me to follow him, when a rock gave way beneath his foot, and he slipped on the wet rock, and fell into the abyss.

The rope held, and the rock beside me held. Calum MacInnes dangled from the end of the rope. He looked up at me, and I sighed, anchored myself by a slab of crag, and I wound and pulled him up and up. I hauled him back onto the path, dripping and cursing.

He said, "You're stronger than you look," and I cursed myself for a fool. He must have seen it on my face for, after he shook himself (like a dog, sending droplets flying), he said, "My boy Calum told me the tale you told him about the Campbells coming for you, and you being sent into the fields by your wife, with them thinking she was your ma, and you a boy."

"It was just a tale," I said. "Something to pass the time."

"Indeed?" he said. "For I heard tell of a raiding party of Campbells sent out a few years ago, seeking revenge on someone who had taken their cattle. They went, and they never came back. If a small fellow like you can kill a dozen Campbells . . . well, you must be strong, and you must be fast."

I must be *stupid*, I thought ruefully, telling that child that tale.

I had picked them off one by one, like rabbits, as they came out to piss or to see what had happened to their friends: I had killed seven of them before my wife killed her first. We buried them in the glen, built a small cairn of stacking stones above them, to weigh them down so their ghosts would not walk, and we were sad: that Campbells had come so far to kill me, that we had been forced to kill them in return.

I take no joy in killing: no man should, and no woman. Sometimes death is necessary, but it is always an evil thing. That is something I am in no doubt of, even after the events I speak of here.

I took the rope from Calum MacInnes, and I clambered up and up, over the rocks, to where the waterfall came out of the side of the hill, and it was narrow enough for me to cross. It was slippery there, but I made it over without incident, tied the rope in place, came down it, threw the end of it to my companion, walked him across.

He did not thank me, neither for rescuing him, nor for getting us across; and I did not expect thanks. I also did not expect what he actually said, though, which was: "You are not a whole man, and you are ugly. Your wife: is she also small and ugly, like yourself?"

I decided to take no offense, whether offense had been intended or no. I simply said, "She is not. She is a tall woman, almost as tall as you, and when she was young—when we were both younger—she was reckoned by some to be the most beautiful girl in the lowlands. The bards wrote songs praising her green eyes and her long red-golden hair."

I thought I saw him flinch at this, but it is possible that I imagined it, or more likely, wished to imagine I had seen it.

"How did you win her, then?"

I spoke the truth: "I wanted her, and I get what I want. I did not give up. She said I was wise and I was kind, and I would always provide for her. And I have."

The clouds began to lower, once more, and the world blurred at the edges, became softer.

"She said I would be a good father. And I have done my best to raise my children. Who are also, if you are wondering, normal-sized."

"I beat sense into young Calum," said older Calum. "He is not a bad child."

"You can only do that as long as they are there with you," I said. And then I stopped talking, and I remembered that long year, and also I remembered Flora when she was small, sitting on the floor with jam on her face, looking up at me as if I were the wisest man in the world.

I was remembering every landmark—climb at the sheep skull, cross the first three streams, then walk along the fourth until the five heaped stones and find where the rock looks like a seagull and walk on between two sharply jutting walls of black rock, and let the slope bring you with it . . .

I could remember it, I knew. Well enough to find my way down again. But the mists confused me, and I could not be certain.

We reached a small loch, high in the mountains, and drank fresh water, caught huge white creatures that were not shrimps or lobsters or crayfish, and ate them raw like sausages, for we could not find any dry wood to make our fire, that high.

We slept on a wide ledge beside the icy water and woke into clouds before sunrise, when the world was grey and blue.

"You were sobbing in your sleep," said Calum.

"I had a dream," I told him.

"I do not have bad dreams," Calum said.

"It was a good dream," I said. It was true. I had dreamed that Flora still lived. She was grumbling about the village boys, and telling me of her time in the hills with the cattle, and of things of no consequence, smiling her great smile and tossing her hair the while, red-golden like her mother's, although her mother's hair is now streaked with white.

"Good dreams should not make a man cry out like that," said Calum. A pause, then, "I have no dreams, not good, not bad."

"No?"

"Not since I was a young man."

We rose. A thought struck me: "Did you stop dreaming after you came to the cave?"

He said nothing.

We walked along the mountainside, into the mist, as the sun came up. The mist seemed to thicken and fill with light, in the sunshine, but did not fade away and I realized that it must be a cloud. The world glowed. And then it seemed to me that I was staring at a man of my size, a small, humpty man, his face a shadow, standing in the air in front of me, like a ghost or an angel, and it moved as I moved. It was haloed by the light, and shimmered, and I could not have told you how near it was or how far away. I have seen miracles and I have seen evil things, but never have I seen anything like that.

"Is it magic?" I asked, although I smelled no magic on the air.

Calum said, "It is nothing. A property of the light. A shadow. A reflection. No more. I see a man beside me, as well. He moves as I move." I glanced back, but I saw nobody beside him.

And then the little glowing man in the air faded, and the cloud, and it was day, and we were alone.

We climbed all that morning, ascending. Calum's ankle had twisted the day before, when he had slipped at the waterfall. Now it swelled in front of me, swelled and went red, but his pace did not ever slow, and if he was in discomfort or in pain it did not show upon his face.

I said, "How long?" as the dusk began to blur the edges of world.

"An hour, less, perhaps. We will reach the cave, and then we will sleep for the night. In the morning you will go inside. You can bring out as much gold as you can carry, and we will make our way back off the island."

I looked at him, then: grey-streaked hair, grey eyes, so huge and wolfish a man, and I said, "You would sleep outside the cave?"

"I would. There are no monsters in the cave. Nothing that will come out and take you in the night. Nothing that will eat us. But you should not go in until daylight."

And then we rounded a rockfall, all black rocks and grey half-blocking our path, and we saw the cave mouth.

I said, "Is that all?"

"You expected marble pillars? Or a giant's cave from a gossip's fireside tales?"

"Perhaps. It looks like nothing. A hole in the rock face. A shadow. And there are no guards?"

"No guards. Only the place, and what it is."

"A cave filled with treasure. And you are the only one who can find it?"

Calum laughed then, like a fox's bark. "The islanders know how to find it. But they are too wise to come here, to take its gold. They say that the cave makes you evil: that each time you visit it, each time you enter to take gold, it eats the good in your soul, so they do not enter."

"And is that true? Does it make you evil?"

". . . No. The cave feeds on something else. Not good and evil. Not really. You can take your gold, but afterwards, things are," he paused, "things are *flat*. There is less beauty in a rainbow, less meaning in a sermon, less joy in a kiss . . ." He looked at the cave mouth and I thought I saw fear in his eyes. "Less."

I said, "There are many for whom the lure of gold outweighs the beauty of a rainbow."

"Me, when young, for one. You, now, for another."

"So we go in at dawn."

"You will go in. I will wait for you out here. Do not be afraid. No monster guards the cave. No spells to make the gold vanish, if you do not know some cantrip or rhyme."

We made our camp, then; or rather we sat in the darkness, against the cold rock wall. There would be no sleep there.

You took the gold from here, as I will do tomorrow. You bought a house with it, a bride, a good name.

Aye, and they meant nothing to me, once I had them, or less than nothing. And if your gold pays for the King over the water to come back to us and rule us and bring about a land of joy and prosperity and warmth, it will still mean nothing to you. It will be as something you heard of that happened to a man in a tale.

I have lived my life to bring the King back. You take the gold back to him. Your King will want more gold, because Kings want more. It is what they do. Each time you come back, it will mean less. The rainbow means nothing. Killing a man means nothing.

Silence then, in the darkness. I heard no birds: only the wind that called and gusted about the peaks like a mother seeking her babe.

We have both killed men. Have you ever killed a woman, Calum MacInnes?

I have not. I have killed no woman, no girls.

I ran my hands over my dirk in the darkness, seeking the wood and center of the hilt, the steel of the blade. It was there in my hands. I had not intended to ever tell him, only to strike when we were out of the mountains, strike once, strike deep, but now I felt the words being pulled from me, would I or never-so.

They say there was a girl. And a thornbush.

If I said a word, I knew, he would be silent on the subject, and never talk about it again. So I said nothing. Only waited.

Calum MacInnes began to speak, choosing his words with care, talking as if he was remembering a tale he had heard as a child and had almost forgotten.

They told me the kine of the lowlands were fat and bonny, and that a man could gain honour and glory by adventuring off to the south and returning with the fine red cattle.

So I went south, and never a cow was good enough, until on a hillside in the lowlands I saw the finest, reddest, fattest cows that a man has ever seen. So I began to lead them away, back the way I had come.

She came after me with a stick. The cattle were her father's, she said, and I was a rogue and a knave and all manner of rough things.

But she was beautiful, even when angry, and had I not already a young wife I might have dealt more kindly to her. Instead I pulled a knife, and touched it to her throat, and bade her stop speaking.

It was another year before I was back that way. I was not after cows that day, but I walked up the side of that bank - it was a lonely spot, and if you had not been looking, you might not have seen it. Perhaps nobody searched for her.

I heard they searched. Although some believed her to be taken by reavers, and others believed her run away with a tinker, or gone to the city. But still, they searched.

Aye. I saw what I did see - perhaps you'd have to have stood where I was standing, to see what I did see. It was an evil thing I did. Perhaps.

Perhaps?

I have taken gold from the cave of the mists. I cannot tell any longer if there is good or there is evil. I sent a message, by a child, at an inn, telling them where she was, and where they could find her.

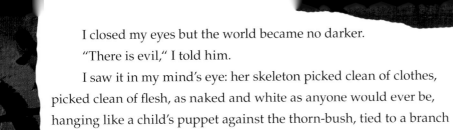

I closed my eyes but the world became no darker.

"There is evil," I told him.

I saw it in my mind's eye: her skeleton picked clean of clothes, picked clean of flesh, as naked and white as anyone would ever be, hanging like a child's puppet against the thorn-bush, tied to a branch above it by its red-golden hair.

At dawn," said Calum MacInnes, as if we had been talking of provisions or the weather, "you will leave your dirk behind, for such is the custom, and you will enter the cave, and bring out as much gold as you can carry. And you will bring it back with you, to the mainland. There's not a soul in these parts, knowing what you carry or where it's from, would take it from you. Then send it to the King over the Water, and he will pay his men with it, and feed them, and buy their weapons. One day, he will return. Tell me on that day that there is evil, little man."

When the sun was up, I entered the cave. It was damp in there. I could hear water running down one wall, and I felt a wind on my face, which was strange, because there was no wind inside the mountain.

In my mind, the cave would be filled with gold. Bars of gold would be stacked like firewood, and bags of golden coins would sit between them. There would be golden chains and golden rings, and golden plates, heaped high like the china plates in a rich man's house.

I had imagined riches, but there was nothing like that here. Only shadows. Only rock.

Something was here, though. Something that waited.

I have secrets, but there is a secret that lies beneath all my other secrets, and not even my children know it, although I believe my wife suspects, and it is this: my mother was a mortal woman, the daughter of a miller, but my father came to her from out of the West, and to the West he returned, when he had had his sport with her. I cannot be sentimental about my parentage: I am sure he does not think of her, and doubt that he ever knew of me. But he left me a body that is small, and fast, and strong; and perhaps I take after him in other ways—I do not know. I am ugly, and my father was beautiful, or so my mother told me once, but I think that she might have been deceived.

I wondered what I would have seen in that cave if my father had been an innkeeper from the lowlands.

You would be seeing gold, said a whisper that was not a whisper, from deep in the heart of the mountain. It was a lonely voice, and distracted, and bored.

"I would see gold," I said aloud. "Would it be real, or would it be an illusion?"

The whisper was amused. *You are thinking like a mortal man, making things always to be one thing or another. It is gold they would see, and touch. Gold they would carry back with them, feeling the weight of it the while, gold they would trade with other mortals for what they needed. What does it matter if it is there or no if they can see it, touch it, steal it, murder for it? Gold they need and gold I give them.*

"And what do you take, for the gold you give them?"

Little enough, for my needs are few, and I am old; too old to follow my sisters into the West. I taste their pleasure and their joy. I feed, a little, feed on what they do not need and do not value. A taste of heart, a lick and a nibble of their fine consciences, a sliver of soul. And in return a fragment of me leaves this cave with them and gazes out at the world through their eyes, sees what they see until their lives are done and I take back what is mine.

"Will you show yourself to me?"

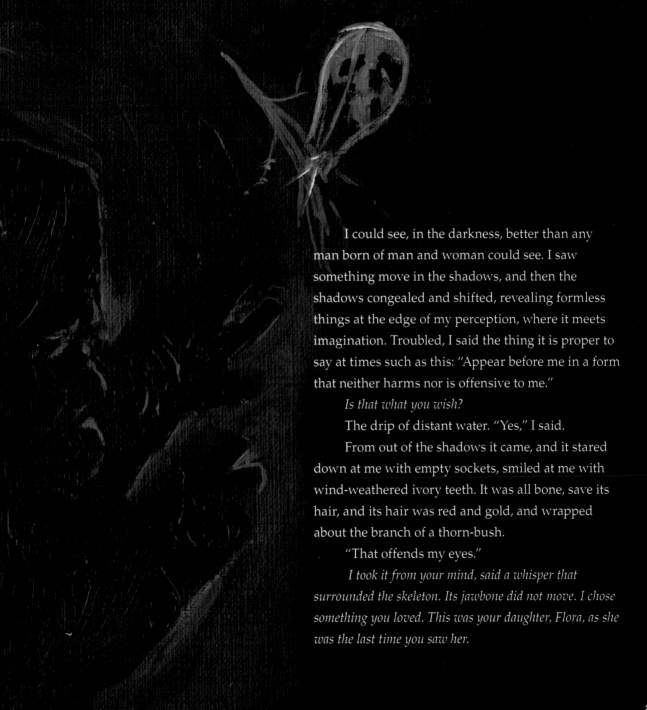

I could see, in the darkness, better than any man born of man and woman could see. I saw something move in the shadows, and then the shadows congealed and shifted, revealing formless things at the edge of my perception, where it meets imagination. Troubled, I said the thing it is proper to say at times such as this: "Appear before me in a form that neither harms nor is offensive to me."

Is that what you wish?

The drip of distant water. "Yes," I said.

From out of the shadows it came, and it stared down at me with empty sockets, smiled at me with wind-weathered ivory teeth. It was all bone, save its hair, and its hair was red and gold, and wrapped about the branch of a thorn-bush.

"That offends my eyes."

I took it from your mind, said a whisper that surrounded the skeleton. Its jawbone did not move. I chose something you loved. This was your daughter, Flora, as she was the last time you saw her.

I closed my eyes, but the figure remained.

It said, *the reaver waits for you at the mouth of the cave. He waits for you to come out, weaponless and weighed down with gold. He will kill you, and take the gold from your dead hands.*

"But I'll not be coming out with gold, will I?"

I thought of Calum MacInnes, the wolf-grey in his hair, the grey of his eyes, the line of his dirk. He was bigger than I am, but all men are bigger than I am. Perhaps I was stronger, and faster, but he was also fast, and he was strong.

He killed my daughter, I thought, then wondered if the thought was mine or if it had crept out the shadows into my head. Aloud, I said, "Is there another way out of this cave?"

You leave the way you entered, through the mouth of my home.

I stood there and did not move, but in my mind I was like an animal in a trap, questing and darting from idea to idea, finding no purchase and no solace and no solution.

I said, "I am weaponless. He told me that I could not enter this place with a weapon. That it was not the custom."

It is the custom now, to bring no weapon into my place. It was not always the custom. Follow me, said the skeleton of my daughter.

I followed her, for I could see her, even when it was so dark that I could see nothing else.

In the shadows it said, *It is beneath your hand.*

I crouched and felt it. The haft felt like bone – perhaps an antler. I touched the blade cautiously in the darkness, discovered that I was holding something that felt more like an awl than a knife. It was thin, sharp at the tip. It would be better than nothing.

"Is there a price?"

There is always a price.

"Then I will pay it. And I ask one other thing. You say that you can see the world through his eyes."

There were no eyes in that hollow skull, but it nodded.

"Then tell me when he sleeps."

It said nothing. It melded into the darkness, and I felt alone in that place.

Time passed. I followed the sound of the dripping water, found a rock pool, and drank. I soaked the last of the oats and I ate them, chewing them until they dissolved in my mouth. I slept and woke and slept again, and dreamed of my wife, Morag, waiting for me as the seasons changed, waiting for me just as we had waited for our daughter, waiting for me forever.

Something, a finger I thought, touched my hand: it was not bony and hard. It was soft, and humanlike, but too cold. *He sleeps.*

I left the cave in the blue light, before dawn. He slept across the cave, catlike, I knew, such that the slightest touch would have woken him. I held my weapon in front of me, a bone handle and a needle-like blade of blackened silver, and I reached out and took what I was after, without waking him.

Then I stepped closer, and his hand grasped for my ankle and his eyes opened.

The wind blew cold on the mountainside. I had danced back, out of his reach, when he had grabbed at me. He stayed on the ground, pushed himself up onto one elbow.

Then he said, "Where is my dirk?"

"I took it," I told him. "While you slept."

He looked at me, sleepily. "And why ever would you do that? If I was going to kill you I would have done it on the way here. I could have killed you a dozen times."

"But I did not have gold then, did I?"

He said nothing.

I said, "If you think you could have got me to bring the gold from the cave, and that not bringing it out would have saved your miserable soul, then you are a fool."

He no longer looked sleepy. "A fool, am I?"

He was ready to fight. It is good to make people who are ready to fight angry.

He rose then, holding a rock in his hand like an axe, and he came at me. I am small, and he could not strike me as he would have struck a man of his own size. He leaned over to strike. It was a mistake.

I held the bone haft tightly, and stabbed upward, striking fast with the point of the awl, like a snake. I knew the place I was aiming for, and I knew what it would do.

He dropped his rock, clutched at his right shoulder. "My arm," he said. "I cannot feel my arm."

He swore then, fouling the air with curses and threats. The dawn light on the mountaintop made everything so beautiful and blue. In that light, even the blood that had begun to soak his garments was purple. He took a step back, so he was between me and the cave. I felt exposed, the rising sun at my back.

"Why do you not have gold?" he asked me. His arm hung limply at his side.

"There was no gold there for such as I," I said.

He threw himself forward, then, ran at me and kicked at me.

My awl blade went flying from my hand. I threw my arms around his leg, and I held on to him as together we tumbled off the mountainside.

His head was above me,
and I saw triumph in it,
and then I saw sky, and
then the valley floor was
above me and I was rising
to meet it and then it
was below me and I was
falling to my death.

Ajar and a bump, and now we were turning over and over on the side of the mountain, the world a dizzying whirligig of rock and pain and sky, and I knew I was a dead man, but still I clung to the leg of Calum MacInnes.

I saw a golden eagle in flight, but below me or above me I could no longer say. It was there, in the dawn sky, in the shattered fragments of time and perception, there in the pain. I was not afraid: there was no time and no space to be afraid in, no space in my mind and no space in my heart. I was falling through the sky, holding tightly to the leg of a man who was trying to kill me; we were crashing into rocks, scraping and bruising and then . . .

. . . we stopped. Stopped with force enough that I felt myself jarred, and was almost thrown off Calum MacInnes and to my death beneath. The side of the mountain had crumbled, there, long ago, sheared off, leaving a sheet of blank rock, as smooth and as featureless as glass. But that was below us. Where we were, there was a ledge, and on the ledge there was a miracle: stunted and twisted, high above the treeline, where no trees have any right to grow, was a twisted hawthorn tree, not much larger than a bush, although it was old. Its roots grew into the side of the mountain, and it was this hawthorn that had caught us in its grey arms.

67

I let go of the leg, clambered off Calum MacInnes's body, and onto the side of the mountain. I stood on the narrow ledge and looked down at the sheer drop. There was no way down from here. No way down at all.

I looked up. It might be possible, I thought, climbing slowly, with fortune on my side, to make it up that mountain. If it did not rain. If the wind was not too hungry. And what choice did I have? The only alternative was death.

A voice: "So. Will you leave me here to die, dwarf?"

I said nothing. I had nothing to say.

His eyes were open. He said, "I cannot move my right arm, since you stabbed it. I think I broke a leg in the fall. I cannot climb with you."

I said, "I may succeed, or I may fail."

"You'll make it. I've seen you climb. After you rescued me, crossing that waterfall. You went up those rocks like a squirrel going up a tree."

I did not have his confidence in my climbing abilities.

He said, "Swear to me by all you hold holy. Swear by your king, who waits over the sea as he has since we drove his subjects from this land. Swear by the things you creatures hold dear— swear by shadows and eagle feathers and by silence. Swear that you will come back for me."

His hair framed his face like a wolf-grey halo. There was red blood on his cheek where he had scraped it in the fall.

I looked up at the rock above us, examined it as best I could. Sometimes good eyes mean the difference between life and death, if you are a climber. I saw where I would need to be as I went, the shape of my journey up the face of the mountain. I thought I could see the ledge outside the cave, from which we had fallen as we fought. I would head for there. Yes.

I blew on my hands, to dry the sweat before I began to climb. "I will come back for you," I said. "With ropes. I have sworn."

"When?" he asked, and he closed his eyes.

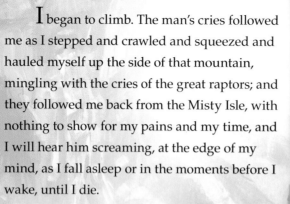

I began to climb. The man's cries followed me as I stepped and crawled and squeezed and hauled myself up the side of that mountain, mingling with the cries of the great raptors; and they followed me back from the Misty Isle, with nothing to show for my pains and my time, and I will hear him screaming, at the edge of my mind, as I fall asleep or in the moments before I wake, until I die.

It did not rain, and the wind gusted and plucked at me but did not throw me down. I climbed, and I climbed in safety.

When I reached the ledge, the cave entrance seemed like a darker shadow in the noonday sun. I turned from it, turned my back on the mountain, and from the shadows that were already gathering in the cracks and the crevices and deep inside my skull, and I began my slow journey away from the Misty Isle. There were a hundred roads and a thousand paths that would take me back to my home in the lowlands, where my wife would be waiting.

There was going to be a festival at the Sydney Opera House, called Graphic, and Jordan Verzar, one of the festival's organizers, asked if I would be interested in reading a story at the Opera House.

The Sydney Opera House is one of the world's iconic places, and I love Australia. I said yes. I sent Jordan an unpublished story about two men walking through a Scotland much like our own in Jacobite times, which I thought would take a little over an hour to read. I suggested Eddie Campbell as the artist to paint pictures to be projected behind me. I've known Eddie Campbell for twenty-five years, and was a fan of his art and his writing before I ever met him as a person. Jordan suggested the FourPlay String Quartet to make music while I read. He sent me their music. I think it was the *Doctor Who* theme that convinced me that they would be perfect.

We rehearsed, modified what we did, performed to a sold-out hall in August 2010, and it was a huge success.

The story was published in an anthology called *Stories,* and it was awarded the Locus Award and the Shirley Jackson Award, both for Best Novelette.

We performed it again in Hobart for the MONA FOMA festival. Eddie created more paintings. I went into the studio with FourPlay a few weeks after this, and recorded myself reading it while they played.

Eddie took the paintings he had already done. He made more art to accompany them. He drew comics. He designed the book you are now holding. It's not pure prose, not a graphic novel. It's a story with pictures unlike anything else I've written.

The Black Mountains are the Black Cuillins in Skye, which is known as the Winged Isle, or perhaps the Misty Isle. There is a cave there, they say, where gold is to be found, and all it will mean if you go there and take some of that gold is that you will become a little more evil . . .

NEIL GAIMAN
JANUARY 2014